DISCOVER THE CREATIVE WORLD OF HOW TO DRAW AND FUN WITH OUR UNIQUE GIFT FOR YOUR KID!

AS AN EXPRESSION OF OUR GRATITUDE FOR YOUR PURCHASE OF OUR BOOK, WE HAVE SOMETHING SPECIAL FOR YOU - A SET OF 30 HOW TO DRAW PAGES THAT WILL AWAKEN YOUR LITTLE ONE'S IMAGINATION AND CREATIVITY.

DON'T MISS THIS UNIQUE OPPORTUNITY TO GIVE YOUR KID MORE THAN JUST A BOOK. DOWNLOAD OUR FREE SET OF 30 HOW TO DRAW NOW AND SEE HOW YOUR KID'S CREATIVITY DEVELOPS. THIS IS OUR WAY TO THANK YOU FOR TRUSTING US AND CHOOSING OUR PRODUCT. THANK YOU AND WE WISH YOU GREAT FUN!

HURRY UP!
THE CODE IS VALID FOR 24 HOURS!

GO TO THE WEB SITE, OR
SCAN THE QR-CODE
www.subscribepage.io/Howtodrawbook

EASTER
COLORING BOOK
FOR BOYS

THIS BOOK
BELONGS TO :

_____

_____

EGG-CRUSHING MONSTER!

EGG-ASSEMBLY LINE ACTIVATED!

DINO-DECORATING WITH ROARSOME!

SAILING THE EGG-SEAS!

DRAGON'S EGG-CITING!

EGG-TREME OFF-ROADING!

EGG-SPRESS LANE!

EGG-PYRAMID CONSTRUCTION ZONE!

DEFENDING EGGS-CALIBUR!

DIVE, DISCOVER, DELIGHT!

EGGS-PRESS LANE CRUISING!

EGG-STARING CONTEST CHAMPION!

EGG-STRAORDINARY AERIAL DROP-OFF!

HOPSTACLE COURSE CREATED!

NINJA EGG-GUARDIAN STANCE!

EGG-STRONAUT ON A SPACE HUNT!

VIKINGS ON AN EGG-SPEDITION!

PLAN FOR EGG-CITEMENT!

SPACECRAFT'S EGG-CELLENT PAYLOAD DROP!

KNIGHT'S EGG-QUISITE TREASURE!

EGG-HAULING IN THE PICKUP!

EGG-TREME HOPPING!

EGG-CITING CRASH-LANDING!

CLIMBING THE EGG-STREME!

EGG-CEPTIONAL SOCCER KICK!

EGG-TRAORDINARY JUGGLE!

ARTISTIC EGG-SPRESSION SESSION!

THE NOBLE EGG!

EGG-CITING HAT TRICK!

EGG-STRA COOL SHADES!

Dear Readers,

Our team would like to thank you sincerely for purchasing our Easter coloring book for boys. Your support and interest in our work are extremely important and inspiring to us.

Your feedback is valuable to us, so We would like to ask you to share your thoughts about the book on the Amazon platform. Your honest reviews will help us better understand what your opinion is about our book and what elements can be improved or changed in the future.

We greatly appreciate every comment, whether it is positive or negative. Your feedback will help other readers make an informed choice when purchasing a book.

Best regards,
Team Simon ColorPress

Made in the USA
Las Vegas, NV
27 March 2024

87789501R00037